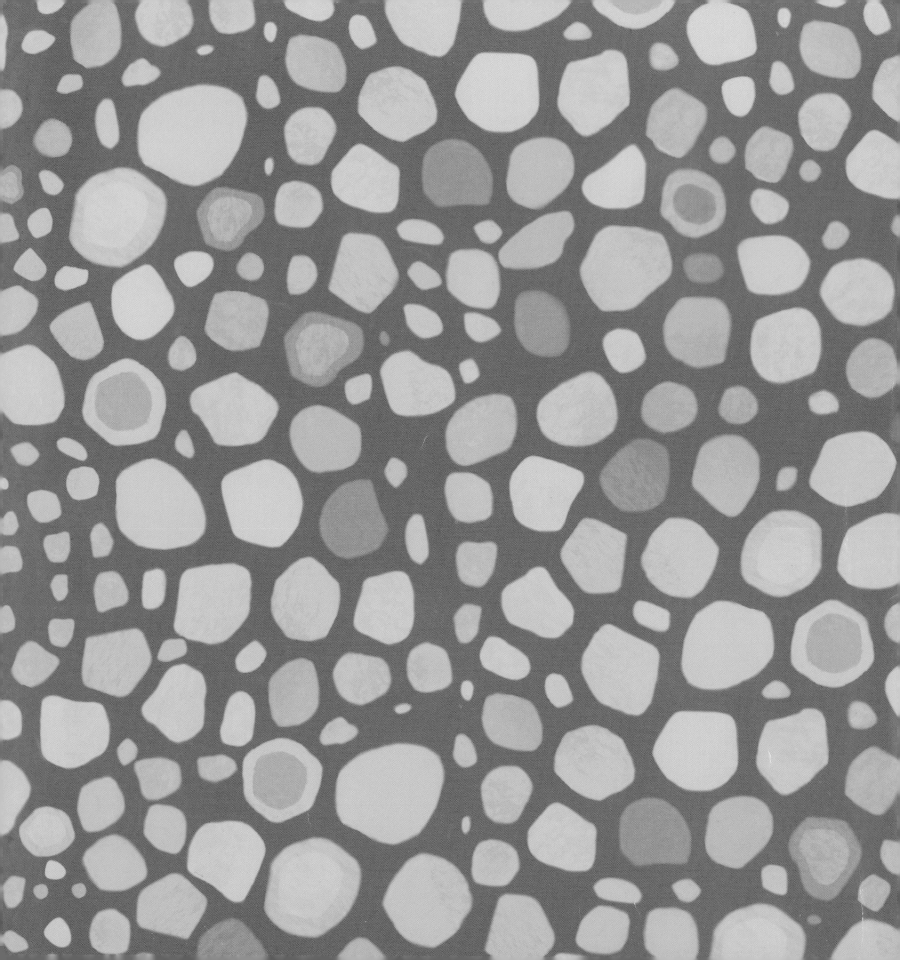

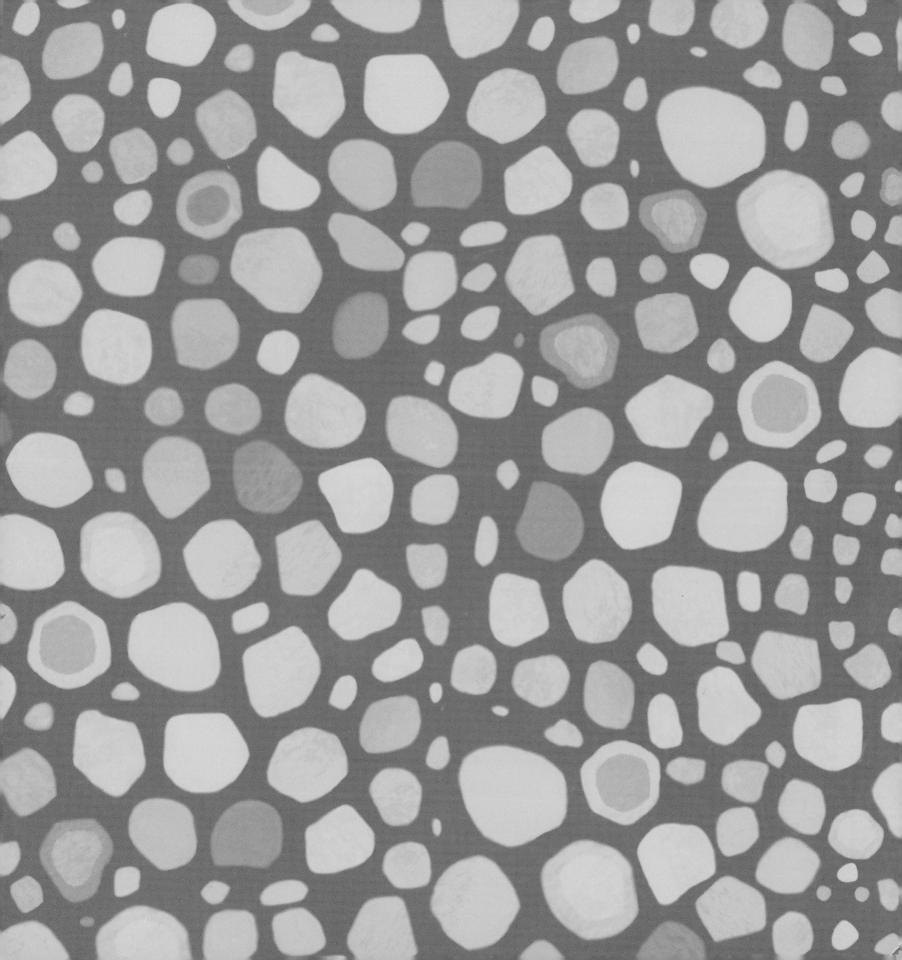

A TEMPLAR BOOK

This book is based on the episode *The Big Mean Green* from the TV series *Gigantosaurus*™.
Screenplay by Alain Vallejo. The TV series *Gigantosaurus*™ is created and produced by
Cyber Group Studios. Based on the original characters created by Jonny Duddle
in the book *Gigantosaurus*, first published by Templar Books in 2014.

First published in the UK in 2022 by Templar Books,
an imprint of Bonnier Books UK
4th Floor, Victoria House,
Bloomsbury Square, London WC1B 4DA
Owned by Bonnier Books
Sveavägen 56, Stockholm, Sweden
www.bonnierbooks.co.uk

1 3 5 7 9 10 8 6 4 2

ISBN 978-1-80078-156-6

Adapted by Samuel Fern
Edited by Harriet Paul and Kirsty Davison
Designed by Ted Jennings
Production by Ché Creasey

Printed in China

GIGANTOSAURUS™

THE BIG MEAN GREEN

templar
books

Rocky, Tiny, Bill and Mazu were
racing through the jungle.

But when they got there, they screeched to a halt.
Steam was rising from the water and
Termy was stuck up a tree!

"HEEELP!" wailed Termy.

"How did you get up there?" Rocky called.

GIGANTO did it!

"What's that?" called a deep voice, as Trey and his friends appeared from the jungle. "Giganto got Termy stuck in that tree?" The other dinosaurs gasped and shook their heads.

That sounds JUST like something he'd do!

"Giganto would NEVER do that!"
Tiny argued, as more dinos gathered.

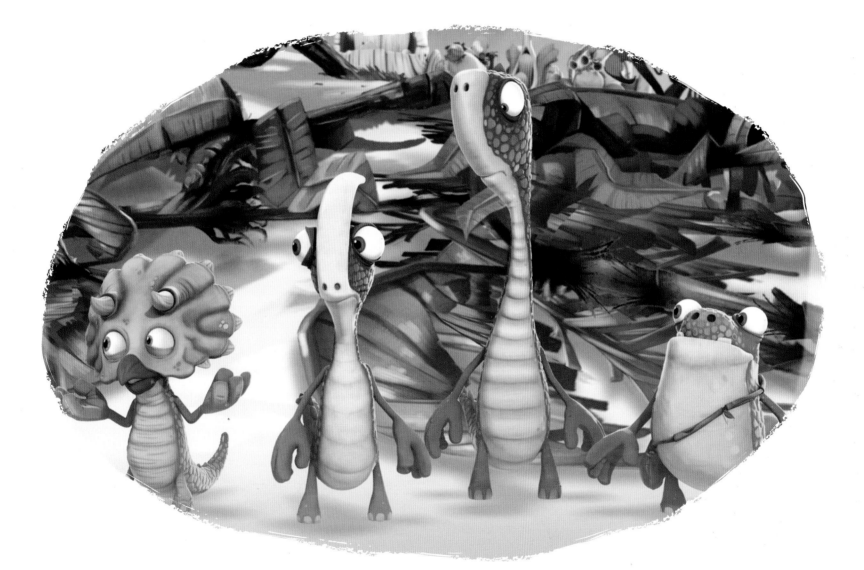

"Termy, did you actually SEE Giganto do it?" Mazu asked.
"Well, no, it was dark," admitted Termy. "But who else could have?"

"What other dino is big enough to lift Termy?" Trey agreed.

Termy giggled and swished her tail, dipping it into the water.

"OWW!" she screamed. "It's too hot!"

"Giganto must've done that too!" said Trey, and the other dinos gasped.

"That's impossible," Rocky protested.

"You're the one who says Giganto can do ANYTHING!" argued Trey.

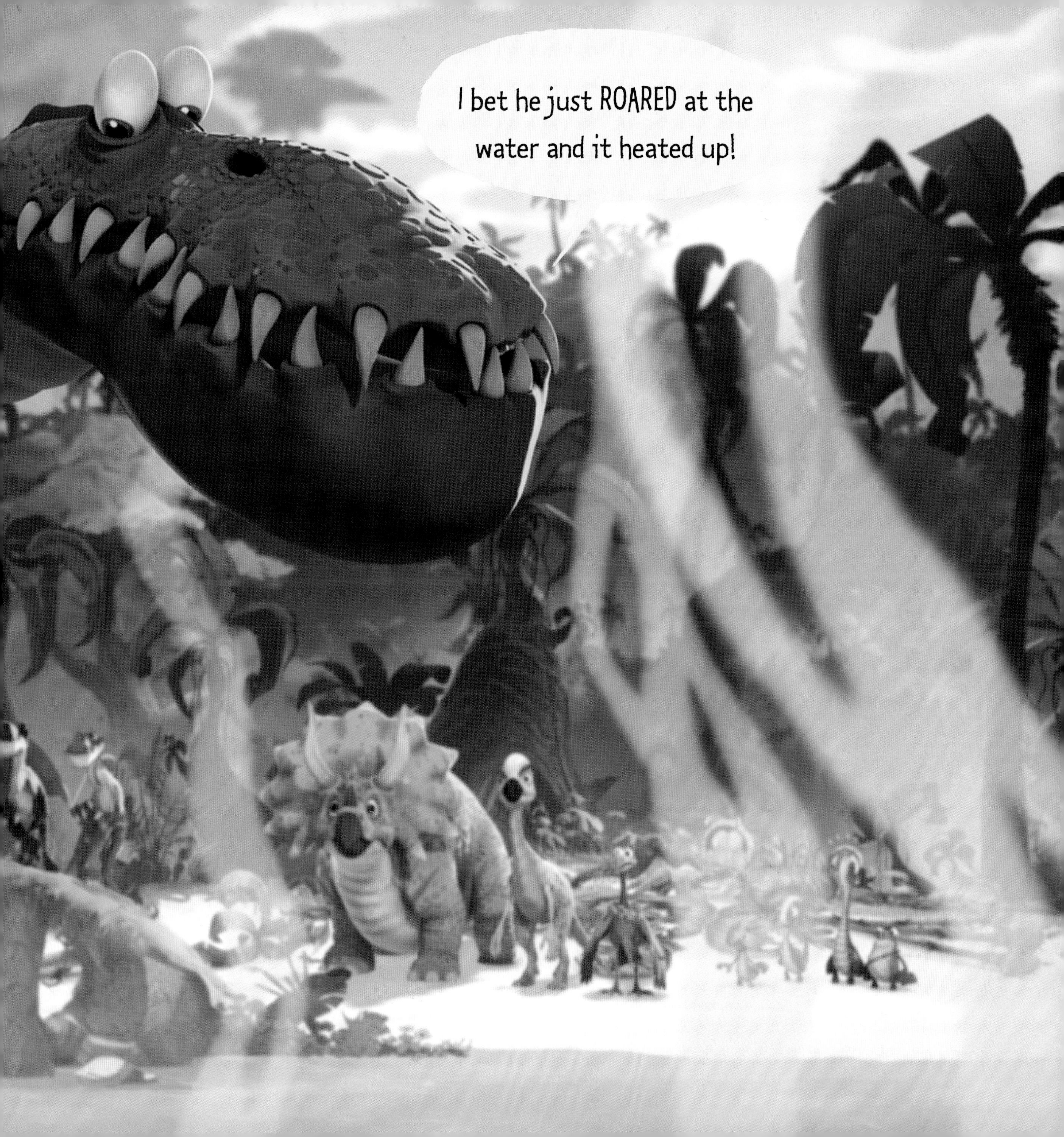
I bet he just ROARED at the water and it heated up!

Just then, Giganto appeared at the other side of the lake.

He took one sniff of the water and stomped off again.

"See?" said Tiny. "He needs the lake to drink. Why would he make it hot?"

"He's always destroying things," said Patchy. "He's ... **THE BIG MEAN GREEN!**"

"We have to protect Cretacia!" Trey announced.
And with that, the angry dinos marched off, chanting . . .

Giganto's got to go! He's being really mean.
We've got to say NO to the big mean green!

"We've got to warn Giganto!" cried Rocky.
"And we need to prove he's innocent!" said Mazu.
So the little dinos split up to try and solve the mystery.

Rocky and Tiny sped across the savannah searching for Giganto. They skidded to a stop when they spotted Rugo.

Have you seen Giganto?

"Giganto?" squeaked Rugo. "We stayed up all
night having a walnut feast together."
"All night?" asked Rocky, scratching his head.
"Then Giganto COULDN'T have put Termy in the tree!"

Last I saw him,
he was heading to the
Frozen Lands . . .

Tiny and Rocky sped off after Giganto before
Trey and the other dinosaurs could find him.

At the lake, Bill and Mazu were investigating the beach, looking for clues that might help clear Giganto's name.

"Keep an eye out for anything unusual," said Mazu as she studied the ground through a magnifying glass.

"What about them?" asked Bill,
pointing at a family of fish in the trees.

"Exactly!" said Mazu. "However the fish ended up there MUST be the same as
what happened to Termy! Maybe we need to try speaking to her again."
Bill gulped and trailed slowly behind Mazu as she headed for the lake.

Tiny and Rocky arrived in the Frozen Lands where they finally caught up to Giganto.
But as they were deciding what to do, the sounds of chanting reached their ears.
The angry dinos were hot on their tails.

Rocky had an idea. He rushed over to a megaphone-shaped block of ice,
took a deep breath and boomed . . .

"Giganto's very polite," said Patchy.

"That's not Giganto!" cried Totor.

"Tiny, is that you?" Trey called.

"Uh oh!" Tiny cried. "We have to warn Giganto!"

Meanwhile, in their boat on the lake, Mazu and Bill floated as close to Termy as they dared to get.

"I'm hungry!" Termy groaned.

"We have some coconuts for you," said Mazu. "But we have some questions first. What were you doing last night?"

"I was sleeping," Termy replied, licking her lips. "Coconut?"

Bill threw one into her mouth.

"Then there was a big splash," Termy continued, "and suddenly I was up in this tree."

Mazu thought for a moment. "Like a wave?"

"Exactly!"

"Thanks, Termy," said Mazu. Bill handed over their last coconut and they sped off before Termy got hungry again!

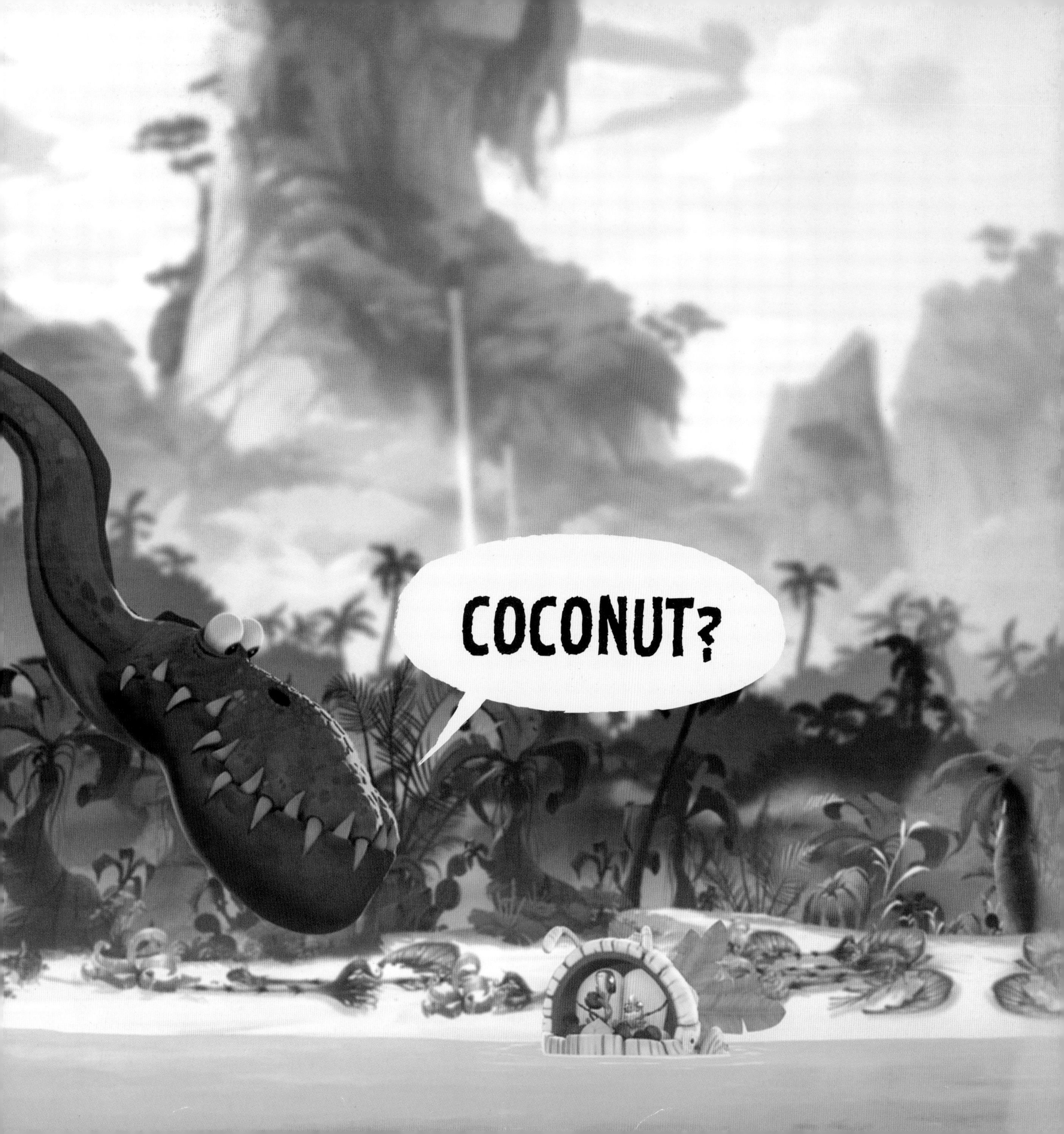
COCONUT?

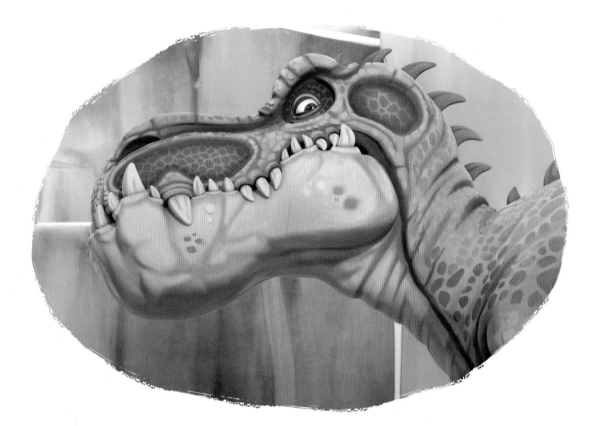

Thankfully, in the Frozen Lands, Rocky and Tiny had managed to get to Giganto before the others.

"You have to go!" Rocky called up to him. Giganto only growled and smashed the ice.

Trey and his friends arrived shouting, "Giganto's got to go!"
Ignoring their cries, Giganto charged at the ice again with a roar.
A loud crack echoed across the Frozen Lands as the ice came loose
and tumbled over the edge of a slippery slope.
Terrified, the dino pack turned and fled back into the jungle.

On the lake, Mazu and Bill had spotted
a patch of bubbles.

Mazu poked her telescope beneath
the surface.

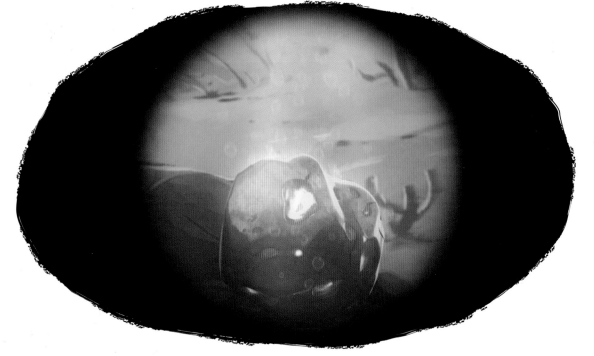

And there sat an enormous fiery rock.
"THAT'S IT!" Mazu cried.

Sure they had solved the mystery, they made their way back to the beach, where they were greeted by Tiny and Rocky.

Trey and the others came crashing out of the jungle. "Giganto's coming!" panted Trey. "We have to stop him."

"Just LISTEN!" Mazu pleaded. "Giganto didn't do any—"

But a thunderous rumble drowned her out . . .

. . . as Giganto and the ice came tumbling down the jungle slope. The little dinos gasped. Had they been wrong? Was Giganto really trying to destroy Cretacia?

But with one mighty push,
Giganto hurled the block of ice into the lake!

The ice melted with a hiss, cooling the water in moments.

Termy carefully dipped a flipper into the water, then dived off the tree and into the lake. She quickly found the hot rock and, with one big throw, hurled it out of the water and onto the beach.

"Where in Cretacia did THAT come from?" gasped Trey.

It's a meteorite!

"A huge rock from outer space. It heated up as it fell,
which then made the water really hot," explained Mazu.
"And made the huge wave that put Termy in the tree!" added Rocky.

Trey shook his head. "Sorry, Giganto! We thought you were the problem but you were just trying to help."

All the dinosaurs cheered:
"He's the **BIG GREEN HERO!**"

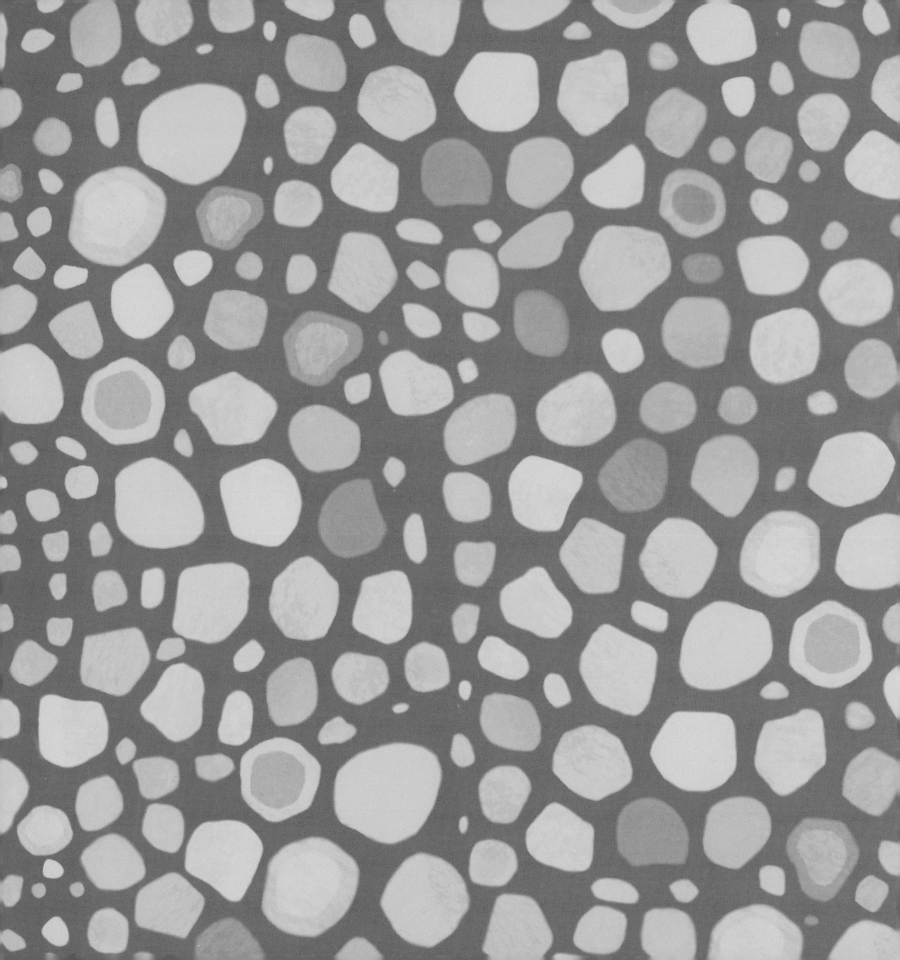

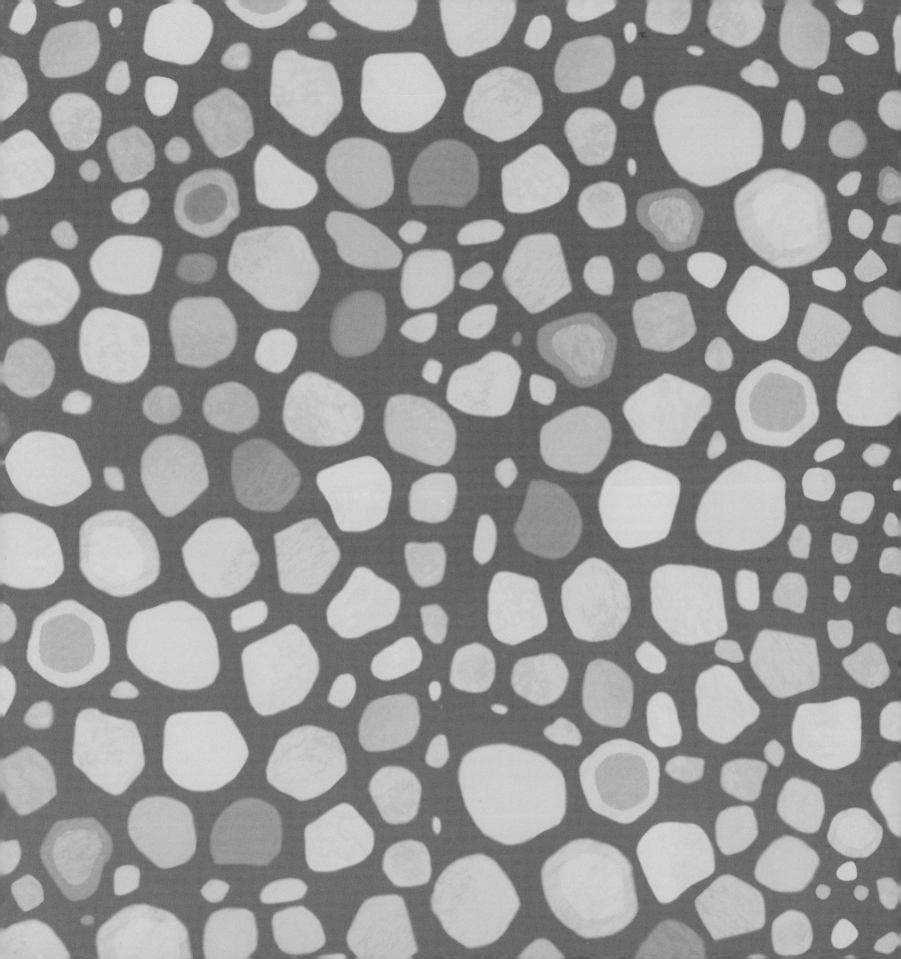

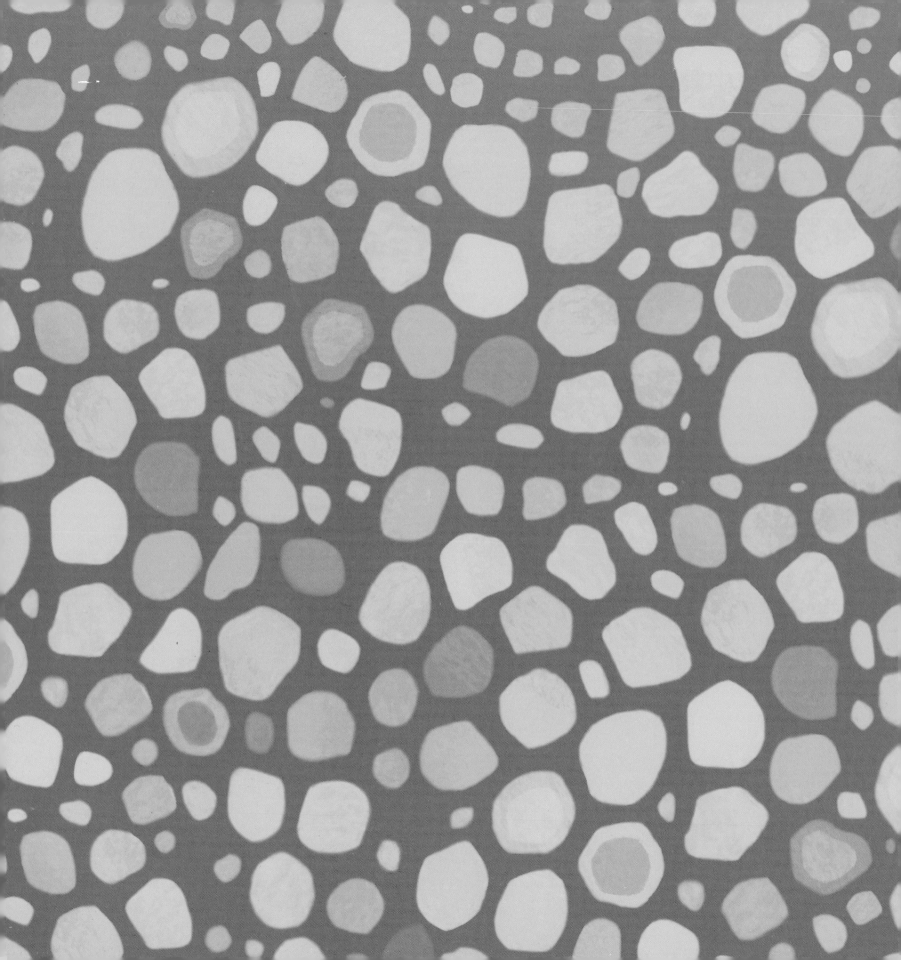